by Fernando Ruiz
illustrated by Marion Eldridge

Printed in the United States of America

ISBN 0-15-317204-5 – Sister Rabbit

Ordering Options
ISBN 0-15-318591-0 (Package of 5)
ISBN 0-15-316985-0 (Grade 1 Package)

4 5 6 7 8 9 10 179 02 01

Big Sister is a rabbit-sitter. Does that mean she sits on little rabbits? No, she doesn't sit on little rabbits.

She sits *for* little rabbits the way a baby-sitter sits for you. That's why she is a called rabbit-sitter!

Most of the time, rabbit-sitting is easy and fun. When Mama Rabbit goes out, she asks Big Sister to watch Little Rabbit.

Big Sister reads to Little Rabbit. She makes Little Rabbit's lunch and plays games with Little Rabbit.

Then Big Sister takes Little Rabbit outside. That is nice for Little Rabbit and Big Sister, too.

One day, Big Sister was playing with Little Rabbit in the yard. They had played tag there before.

Big Sister started to laugh. She thought Little Rabbit was funny. Then, Big Sister did not laugh. She couldn't find Little Rabbit!

Big Sister looked here.

Big Sister looked there.

Big Sister looked just about everywhere!

Big Sister still could not find Little Rabbit. Then Little Rabbit popped out!

"There you are!" said Big Sister. "You funny little bunny! Now I will carry you inside. You can run to your bed for a nap!"

Teacher/Family Member

Hide-and-Seek

Ask your child to tell where Little Rabbit was hiding in the story. Then look in nature books and magazines to find out where real rabbits hide.

School-Home Connection

Invite your child to read Sister Rabbit to you. Then ask your child to tell whether he or she liked the story and to explain why or why not.

Word Count:	193
Vocabulary Words:	most nice before laugh thought carry
Phonic Elements:	Long Vowel: /ē/y, ie easy funny everywhere bunny

TAKE-HOME BOOK

Welcome Home

Use with "Lilly's Busy Day."